Be Good to Each Other

OTHER BOOKS BY LOWELL ERDAHL

Unwitting Witnesses
Preaching for the People

Be Good to Each Other

AN OPEN LETTER ON MARRIAGE

Lowell and Carol Erdahl

HAWTHORN BOOKS, INC.
Publishers/New York

To Becki, Paul, and Beth

Scripture quotations are from the Revised Standard Version of the Bible, copyrighted 1946, © 1971 by the Division of Education and Ministry of the National Council of the Churches in the United States of America. The Dietrich Bonhoeffer quotation is from *Letters and Papers from Prison*, rev. ed., originally published as *Prisoner for God*, ed. Eberhard Bethge (New York: Macmillan, 1967), p. 49. The Jess Lair quotation is from *I Ain't Much, Baby, But I'm All I've Got* (Greenwich, Conn.: Fawcett, 1974), p. 174.

Contents

Introduction

This book is an expanded version of a letter that we sent to Carol's nephew, John Syvertsen, and his bride, Pamela Edwards, on the occasion of their marriage. It is the longest letter we have ever written, exceeding in length even the longest letters of the apostle Paul. We readily acknowledge that St. Paul was not only more brief, but also more profound than we have been able to be, but at the same time we believe there is at least a slight parallel between what we have written to Pam and John and what Paul wrote to the Christians at Rome and other places. We, too, have sought to share a gift which we hope will be a source of strength and a means toward joy. Being unable to share this gift in person, we, like Paul, chose to put our thoughts in the form of a letter which enabled us to be personal and yet somewhat comprehensive.

This is, however, no attempt for a final word on marriage. It is one married couple's personal thoughts shared with our nephew and his bride. Since distance kept us from knowing either of them intimately, what we have written may be as meaningful to persons unknown to us as we hope it has been for them. In this spirit, we share our thoughts, hopeful that they may help persons, married or soon to be, find greater joy in the exciting and often perilous venture of life together.

After sending this letter to Pam and John, we made a few copies to share with some friends and to give to couples being married in our church. The response frankly surprised us and resulted in additional copies being run for use in a marriage enrichment series in our congregation and for a marriage counseling course at Luther Theological Seminary. On the basis of these experiences, we are bold to suggest that in addition to being a book for personal reading and for a wedding, anniversary, Christmas, or birthday gift, *Be Good to Each Other* can also be used by pastors and counselors as an aid in premarital and marriage counseling, in marriage enrichment series in churches, and in seminary courses and pastoral seminars preparing students and clergy for more effective counseling.

In order to help facilitate the kind of communication we believe essential to meaningful marriage, an appendix of questions and thoughts for reflection and discussion has been added. Our hope is that these thoughts and questions will be used by couples in personal discussion with each other and that they will also provide a concrete basis for group discussion in church groups and counseling classes.

All will not agree with everything we have written, but we hope that the reading of it will stimulate reflection and communication, and if some through these pages find more meaning in marriage, we will be grateful.

Dear Pam and John

Dear Pam and John:

As you begin your venture of marriage, we want to give you a very personal gift. We have never shared a gift in this way before, but we do so now in the hope that it will be meaningful to you. We would like to tell you of some of our experiences in marriage and we wish to share a little of what our years of married life have taught us.

Although we have known you all your life, John, and enjoyed meeting you, Pam, we really don't know either of you very well. Space has kept us apart, but we hope that these thoughts will help to bring us closer together and that they will encourage you to live more intimately and joyfully with one another.

We Wish You Joy

Our wish for you is joy abounding through all your years together. This joy we wish for you includes, but goes beyond, fun and happiness. It is also the joy of tender intimacy shared in body, mind, and spirit. Freedom has a place in it—freedom to grow as persons as well as a couple. Through this joy runs a sense of meaning that springs from resources to live from and purposes worth living for. All these, and whatever more goes into joy in fullness, we wish for you.

Our hope and prayer for you is that a long time from now you will be able to look back across your years together with an abundance of gratitude and a minimum of regret. Even at best there is, in each of our lives, plenty to regret—all those acts of word and deed that should, or should never have been. After over twenty years together we have memories enough of things we now wish had been different, but in spite of all that, we remain deeply grateful for having shared this time together. Such gratitude seems to us the most true sign of joy. So may your adventure of life together lead increasingly to thankfulness that tells of joy.

We Promise You Trouble

But lest there be any misunderstanding, we must go on at once to promise you trouble. We don't know exactly what you expect of marriage, but on the basis of our experience, we will risk a double prediction. First, that you will have many times in your marriage when you are so tender, warm, loving, and affectionate that you will believe it impossible for you ever again to have an unkind thought or feeling toward each other. Second, that there will also be times when you are so angry, hurt, and resentful you will wonder how you could ever have loved each other at all. On the occasion of his golden wedding anniversary, one of our uncles confided that, "During all these fifty years, we have never thought of separation or divorce, but we have on occasion thought of murder." That, too, has been our experience and to acknowledge it is not to report a bad marriage. It is, however, to confess a relationship in which affection and anger, joy and resentment, fun and frustration follow and precede each other within the changing cycles of intimacy. So when trouble comes, please don't think quickly of separation or divorce and certainly don't yield to the temptation of murder. Having problems doesn't necessarily mean that you have an unsatisfactory marriage; it can mean that you have an intimate marriage.

A friend once told us, "It's terrible to be married." He defended this statement by pointing to some of the heavy responsibilities and the limits of freedom that marriage involves and told of resentments and misunderstandings that can make marriage miserable. But then, lest we get the wrong impression, he went on to say, "It's also wonderful to be married. It is the most meaningful, joyful relationship that I have ever had and I would not change it for anything." We have often thought of how his experience is equally true in other ways. It is both terrible and wonderful to be single; there are miseries and joys in the single life. So also with being human, it is both terrible and wonderful to be alive in this world. Across the years both gloom and gladness are part of every person's experience.

Marriage Can't Do Everything

We know from our experience that living together has great potential to create changes for both better and worse. Because we are so important to each other, we do more than anyone else to lift or depress each other's moods. Marriage solves some problems but creates others. Someone has said that "Half the troubles of life come from being single, and the other half from being married" and we certainly understand the point of that, but think it's not quite true. In terms of percentages, which are at best only suggestive, it seems to us more likely that about one fourth of the problems come from being single and one fourth from being married, with the other fifty percent coming from our being persons alive in a world like this. That is to say, we think that at least half our troubles have little to do with whether we are single or married. They are just part of what is involved in being human. Failure to recognize this fact may be one of the most significant contributors to unhappy and broken marriages.

When we get married it's easy to dream of marriage as the solution to all our problems. But in reality this dream is an illusion. Getting married will, hopefully, solve some problems, but it will not automatically free us from the troubles that come with being human. We still have to face the routines of daily living and are still as susceptible as ever to the basic anxieties of existence which remind us that we are not gods, but human beings—frail, finite, fallible, one day soon or late to die.

Those who get married in the hope of being freed from all the anxieties of human existence are, therefore, certain to be disappointed. When the realities of married life destroy this dream, they may think that the fault is in this particular marriage and begin to fantasize over being married to someone else who could make the dream come true. There are, of course, mistaken marriages and for some the "second time around" is more beautiful than the first, but when this is so, one reason may be that it is entered into with more realistic expectations. But the fact remains that neither getting married, nor getting divorced, nor getting remarried solves the most basic problems of human life. They will be present in whatever state we live. A good marriage will, of course, help to make them easier to bear and a bad marriage will likely make them seem even worse, but for all of that, let's neither blame everything on, nor credit everything to, marriage. The fault, or source of blessing, often lies not in our marital state, but in ourselves and in our wider world.

To stress that marriage can't do everything is not to deny its immense potential for good. The fact of being legally bound to each other, so that we cannot call off the relationship on a moment's notice, is in itself a facilitator of more joy than misery. The legal obligations about which we may complain keep us together through troubled times enabling us again to be renewed in love. We believe that Dietrich Bonhoeffer overstates the case when he says, "It is not your love that sustains the marriage, but from now on, the marriage that sustains your love." Our marriage is certainly sustained by our love; but the reverse is also true, our love is sustained by our marriage.

All in all, we much prefer the troubles of being married to those of being single and would gladly do it all over again. Our getting married has been one of the best things we ever did, and we hope that twenty years from now you will say the same.

Forewarned Is Forearmed

We hope that you expect great gladness in your life together. Joy waits to sustain you and to surprise you. But to be forewarned of difficult days can help you see your marriage in a more mature perspective.

Whether single or married there will always be some hard times ahead. Accepting the fact that life will not always be easy can strangely help to make things a lot easier for us. For example, understanding that the "model" teenager is often a bit rebellious can help parents live more comfortably through those turbulent years. In the same way awareness that the "model" marriage includes the rhythms of up and down which are part of being human, as well as the inevitable conflicts that come with closeness, helps us to roll with the punches and to recover more quickly than is otherwise possible. Human life is for each of us an often lonely voyage on a restless and sometimes stormy sea. We are tremendously grateful that we can sail together, but have learned that our love does not shield us from every turbulent wind and wave.

When you encounter your first serious conflicts and see each other at your worst, you will be tempted to say, "Now I see what you are really like! You are mean and selfish." But just wait a minute! You will have se   and said the truth. All of us are mean and selfish. That's   fact of life for each of us. It's true, but it's not all the truth. That isn't all that we are "really like." We are also loving and kind. We are capable of great love as well as of great hatred. To face that double fact in ourselves as well as in our partner is a step toward mature intimacy.

Our most happy moments are saddened by an awareness that "this time of ecstasy will pass." Occasions of deepest communion with one another will be followed sooner or later by times of conflict and misunderstanding. But the other side is also true. Times of resentment and coldness will be followed also by reconciliation and warm renewal. It's been said that "married couples go from th   world war to the boudoir" and vice versa. Those transiti   s don't always happen quickly, but that they do happen is an indication of the dynamic changes of attitude and action   hat are part of the living relationship of married life.

Share What Is Deepest

In his book, *I Ain't Much, Baby, But I'm All I've Got*, Jess Lair says, "The most loving thing we can do is tell it like it is with us in our deepest hearts." Someone also has said, "To love is to give yourself to someone else." Those definitions go together. To tell what is in our deepest hearts is to give ourselves to someone else.

In our experience, the deepest intimacy of marriage is not just the intimacy of sexual relations. They are a wonderful and vital part of total intimacy. Praise God for this beautiful gift. But even more intimate than the physical closeness of sexual relations is the mental and emotional sharing of mind and heart. To share what is in the depth of mind and heart, to confide our hopes and fears, doubts and dreams is intimacy at its best.

Such sharing is often painful and sometimes embarrassing. The depths contain thoughts of dread and disappointment which we do not like to admit to ourselves or to confide to someone else. Many of the things that bother us seem to our rational side to be either too personal or too insignificant to talk about. We may think we are too big to be upset by such things. But our feelings are not ruled by our minds, and the only way to clear the air and renew the relationship is often to talk it out. Talk can be cheap, but it can also be priceless. To share the negative as well as the positive is the painful price of intimacy. As we do so, we experience the truth of the old saying, "When we share our joys we double them; when we share our troubles we cut them in half."

"He Doesn't Talk to Me"

A wife once told of her problem in marriage. She first bragged about her husband. He was an excellent provider and was faithful and kind. He was good with the children and she had no doubt of his love. "There is just one little thing," she said, "he doesn't talk to me." Subsequent conversation revealed that wasn't literally true. He did talk about some things. He said, "Please pass the potatoes," and "What movie would you like to see tonight?" He talked about painting the house and going to the ball game, but he did not share what was in his deepest heart. He didn't confide his personal thoughts or feelings. As the months and years passed, she began to feel as if she were living with a stranger.

Sharing in depth seems especially difficult for some people who have been brought up in families where they keep everything to themselves. Some men seem to feel that the telling of personal thoughts and feelings is a sign of weakness or a threat to their manhood. Even to say, "I love you" is to confess the need of another person, which some, in their fear of becoming dependent, find difficult to do.

Yet whatever our patterns of past isolation may be, something in us yearns for a relationship in which we can be open and honest with each other. While inhibitions keep us from sharing freely, yearnings for intimacy invite us to risk saying something that will help break the defensive wall that keeps us a lonely stranger separated from the one we love.

There are ways in which these defenses can be broken. The woman who complained that "he doesn't talk to me" told her husband of her anguish and was surprised that he was open to visiting with a third person, in whose presence they were able to make a new beginning in their relationship. She learned that there were some ways in which she contributed to her husband's silence and others by which she made it easier for him to be more open. We sometimes encourage and enable the very behavior and attitudes in each other which we most dislike. We may, for example, complain of the silent partner and yet so ridicule his or her feeble attempts at sharing that he or she is put down into retreating to a safer solitude. Or, while complaining of too much nagging and bickering, we do all sorts of things that continue to provoke it.

Let's Talk about It

If you are having difficulty sharing, here are two communication starters which some have found helpful.

The first deals with personal role expectations. Each of us expects certain things of ourselves and of our spouses. Some of these are more important than others. To help each other know what matters most to you, try arranging the following items in order of importance:

__to help earn the family income
__to help with responsibilities for meals and housekeeping
__to help seek common recreational and cultural interests
__to be a satisfying sexual partner
__to help maintain good relations with relatives and friends

__to help care for the children

__to be a personal companion

__to promote correct religious faith and values

__to help manage the family finances

__to take a leadership role in community and social activities

__to assume the major responsibility for making family decisions

Make two lists. In the first, list them in order of importance for yourself; in the second, in terms of what you expect of your spouse. Don't attempt to guess what you think your partner's order of importance will be. Let your spouse do that for himself or herself. Put them in the order of importance to you.

Do this ranking independently of each other. Add other areas that are important to you; then get together to compare and talk about the things that are most significant to each of you and why. This is not a test. Try to be as honest and open as possible. If your number one expectation of your spouse is his or her number ten expectation of self, you had better face the difference and seek mutually satisfying accommodation or compromise.

We don't have to agree on everything but we do need to come to terms with our differences. One of you can like western music while the other prefers classics, but if you have only one stereo you can't play both at the same time. "Open marriage" at its best gives each partner freedom to be oneself and, at the same time, respects the limits of freedom inherent in a relationship of love. Speaking of the relationships of love between husband and wife, parents and children, a wife and mother once said, "We hold each other tightly with an *open* hand." To us that open hand is a beautiful symbol of love which does hold tightly, but does not stifle or enslave.

"Honey, I . . ."

As another conversation starter, try playing some of the "Honey, I . . ." games. There are many possible variations such as, "Honey, I'm glad . . . ," "Honey, I wish . . . ," "Honey, I'm grateful . . . ," "Honey, I'm sorry . . . ." In each case try to complete the sentence in several different ways and then share your sentences with each other and talk about why you feel as you do. With the "Honey, I wish . . ." game, be sure to seek specific ways by which some of your wishes may come true. Perhaps you can trade the fulfillment of one wife's wish for one husband's. Such trading may not seem very romantic (depending on the specific wishes), but it is a vital part of civilized living together.

As your communication deepens you will discover both your differences and your similarities. You will sometimes be surprised that you both feel rejected or dominated by each other. When you find yourself saying, "What do you mean? You are the one who's been ignoring me!" you have discovered a common feeling which can help you grow in your understanding of each other. By exploring this shared feeling together, you can further deepen your relationship.

Say It and Hear It

When we husbands and wives fail to understand each other it is likely because we are delinquent in either speaking or listening, or both. We may, for example, complain of being misunderstood and yet be to blame ourselves for having shared so little that sufficient understanding is impossible. When meeting with couples for marital counseling, it is common to hear one say to the other, "I never knew you felt that way" or "Why didn't you tell me that before?" It would often be helpful to be able to read each other's minds, but until we have developed that art more fully, we need to speak our minds and hearts.

On the other hand, it is of course true that speaking produces no understanding until it is heard. Most of us are probably better at speaking than listening. If this is true for us, we need to be reminded of the old saying, "The good Lord has given each of us two ears and one mouth and we should take the hint." Too often we talk much and hear little, and even when silent are more preoccupied with what we are planning to say next than attentive to what the other is saying. So when we complain that we don't, or can't, understand our partners, the fault again may be in ourselves for failing to really hear what is being clearly expressed.

Speech and hearing are great gifts, but are of no value until they are used. We need not spend half our lives feeling sorry for ourselves for being misunderstood or for being incapable of understanding each other. As we have mouths to speak and ears to hear, we can use them. Take time to verbalize and if that doesn't come naturally, prepare a little speech or write a letter. Take time to listen with attention and concern for what is really being said and if it is not clear ask, "What do you mean?" When we do so, we are often surprised at what we learn, but more than that, we help each other to fulfill one of our deepest human needs— the need to be understood.

When we listen we may discover that we hear some things over and over and will often be tempted to shut off the conversation with a sarcastic "You told me that before." But why do these things keep coming up? Is it because we possibly still haven't heard them and that they are expressive of a very significant meaning? This may be especially true of memories from our childhoods. These may seem like meaningless incidents but there are reasons why they keep coming to mind and why we feel it necessary to share them with someone else. When we tell these memories, we are really saying, "I want you to know me and to understand why I am as I am."

The Wrong Fears

There are, of course, things we are afraid to share because we do not wish to burden each other. Perhaps we have troubles at work, but to tell about them would cause worry and anxiety. There are times when we must keep things to ourselves, yet not to share them may create a feeling of lonely isolation. The most difficult burden of all may be the sense of separation that comes when we are aware that our spouse is troubled, but does not trust or respect us enough to share it.

At other times we decline from sharing for fear that we will break down and reveal our weakness. Perhaps we will start to cry and expose ourselves to ridicule, so we don't dare talk about it. We clam up and cry on the inside or when we are alone, which is probably far better than not at all. In our society, men are especially inhibited in this regard, but if in our liberated world women are learning to be more honest in asserting their minds and wills, men can also be liberated to be more honest in expressing their emotions. Tears and laughter are gifts of God and when there is something to cry or laugh about, it is well to cry and to laugh.

Our trouble is often that we are afraid of the wrong things. We are afraid to show our emotions, while it is the hiding of our emotions that keeps us from meeting and understanding each other. We are afraid that our walls of defense will fall down, while it is these very walls that separate us from one another. To share times of tears as well as laughter is part of the pain and joy of intimacy.

We all yearn for a marriage relationship in which we can be totally open and honest with each other and should do all we can to make such sharing possible. But we also need to remember that honesty isn't everything. We need to be kind as well as truthful. In kindness we will sometimes choose to keep some truth to ourselves. When, for example, we meet someone more beautiful or more handsome than our spouse, we don't need to rush home declaring, "I wish you were as good-looking as so-and-so I met today." It might be true, but it certainly would not be kind. We are to speak "the truth in love" and are also to "be kind to one another, tenderhearted" (Ephesians 4:15, 32).

What Are You Trying to Tell Me?

Even couples who seldom verbalize their deepest thoughts and feelings are still constantly communicating with each other. Their attitudes and actions speak more loudly than their words. Almost everything we do or say has some meaning if we can only see or hear what it is. You have probably heard the old story of the farmer who rushed across the field to ask his neighbor why he was beating his mule. "I'm not beating him," the neighbor replied, "I'm just trying to get his attention." In similar ways we do all sorts of things to get each other's attention, and if we realize this is going on, we can be much more understanding and considerate of each other's behavior and attitudes.

One of us was once present when another couple were having an intense argument. The wife was especially vicious in berating her husband. When asked, "What are you trying to tell him?" her mood changed abruptly and she began to cry. Through the tears she blurted out, "I just wish that once in a while he'd take me in his arms and tell me that he loves me." It seems safe to say that until that moment her husband was not getting the message. All he heard was anger and resentment, yet all the while his wife was really pleading for love.

We may criticize this wife for not simply saying to her husband, "Tell me that you love me," but when we think about it we know why she was reluctant to do so. She lived in the hope that he would say it without being asked. Had he come home and given her a big hug after having been asked, she would have thought, "You're only doing it because I asked you." Having waited so long, it was only in painful desperation that she could finally blurt it out. Had they sometime before, when the emotional pitch was less intense, been able to share their mutual longings, perhaps in a setting like that of the "Honey, I wish . . ." game, it might have been possible to avoid reaching this terrible impasse.

We urge you to listen for the sounds of the heart as well as the lips and to look behind your actions for their possible meanings. Ask each other, "What are you trying to tell me?" When you do, we think you will often discover what someone has called "the soul of goodness" behind the appearance of things that look evil. Our worst words and most hurtful behavior are often really cries and acts of desperation which rise from God-given but frustrated yearnings for love and life.

Accentuate the Positive

When we were young there was a popular song with the title "Ac-cent-tchu-ate the Positive" that urged accentuation of the affirmative and elimination of the negative. We don't think it is either wise or possible to eliminate all negative thoughts and do not advocate a Pollyanna approach to life. At the same time, we have learned that it is better to accentuate the positive than harp on the negative.

A wise coach was once asked why he did so little complaining about the team's mistakes and so much bragging about their good plays. His answer was direct and to the point: "I have discovered that complaining doesn't do much good and that commending does much to create a better team." So also with life in general. Who are the people who have most influenced your life for good? Are they persons who have given you the most negative criticism or those who have provided the most positive encouragement?

Imagine a marriage in which negative comments abound: "Why can't you ever be on time?" "Don't you know how to do anything right?" "You are about as sexless as they come!" What effect do you think such comments have on improving punctuality, household repairs, and sexual fulfillment? If anything, they are likely to create resentment that makes everything worse.

Imagine another marriage in which the couple make a point of sharing positive appreciation. An honestly spoken "I am glad you are home early" or "The bedroom looks beautiful; I didn't know you could paint so well" and a tenderly whispered, "I think you are very sexy" will do more to encourage the same behavior than will a month of griping.

Reading this you may be thinking, "Wait a minute; in the one marriage things were terrible, so there was nothing to be positive about, while in the other all was well, so it was natural to be appreciative." Maybe, but also maybe not. How did these marriages get this way? They may have begun with similar circumstances, but negative harping created resentment which reinforced negative behavior in the one, while positive appreciation encouraged positive behavior in the other.

To urge accentuation of the positive is not to advocate dishonesty or manipulative game playing, but rather, to promote honest expression of heartfelt appreciation. The positive couple didn't just pretend or make up things for which to be grateful. When they saw a good thing, they were simply honest and kind enough to acknowledge it. Even when a couple are coexisting in a state of cold war isolation, they usually continue to be halfway civilized toward each other so that there are some things for which to be rightly grateful. If each would be honest enough to confess a little thankfulness such as "That was really a good dinner" or "Thanks for picking up the back hall," there might be a breakthrough toward a much better life together.

Being properly positive also means having the kindness to express complaints with some measure of civilized tact and to realize that there are times when complaints had better be at least temporarily kept to oneself. An insightful woman told of visiting a psychotherapist seeking help in dealing with her parents-in-law, with whom she and her husband were living. He advised her to be more open in expressing her feelings, whereupon she proceeded to "tell off" both her husband and her in-laws. Having done so, she soon discovered the problem to be worse than ever. An angry husband and a couple of bewildered and rejected parents were still there to be dealt with. Fortunately, they all had the maturity to face the situation and make a new beginnning. Their experience should not lead us to bottle everything up, but it can remind us that impulsively blowing our stacks is often less than an automatic cure for all our problems.

Marry a Good Friend

Ann Landers urges people looking toward a meaningful lifelong relationship to "marry a good friend." Being good friends may be an insufficient basis for marriage, but friendship does seem to us necessary for a lasting relationship of mutual understanding and joy. To say this is not to minimize the romantic side of marriage. Few would doubt the wisdom of being married to a person with whom we enjoy going to bed, but some seem less concerned about that person also being one with whom we enjoy getting up in the morning. One of our reservations about premarital sex is that it can easily short-circuit the relationship so that while there may be much passion, there is little chance for the development of friendship. Passion and friendship seem to us best kept together. The combined sharing of the heart, mind, and body enriches intimacy at every level.

Our writing to you now about marrying a good friend may seem inappropriate. Whatever your motives for courtship, you are now getting married, so isn't it a bit late to think of these things? We don't think so. Even if passion has overshadowed friendship thus far, it is not too late to become good friends. Friendship begins and thrives as it is nurtured by sharing mutual concerns, and it enhances rather than diminishes the potential for passionate fulfillment.

We certainly have days when we are our worst enemies but are immensely grateful that on most days we are able to name each other as "my best friend." There is no magic way in which this happens; it is part of the overall effect of everything we think, do, feel, and say. Remember especially that friendship is based on *mutual* respect. Some marriages seem founded upon neurotic dependencies rather than mutual respect. One may, for example, feel sorry for the other and mistake the sense of being needed for being in love. The other may worship the needed one as a kind of savior without whom he or she believes it is impossible to live. Having pity is often a virtue, but it is a very poor basis for marriage. Making a "god" of another person is also to set the stage for certain disillusionment.

No one can be a god to anyone else, and it is both disastrous and idolatrous to attempt to do so. As God does not take the place of a person who dies, but leaves an empty place, as if in tribute to that person's importance, so also a spouse does not take the place of God; nor for that matter of other people and the rest of creation. We can't be "gods" or "saviors" for each other, but we can be friends sharing our lives as human beings who both respect and need, but do not worship or rely solely upon, each other. Being someone, but not everything to each other, we live in a mutuality of healthy interdependence in which we feel free to give and receive without either demeaning or idolizing.

There are, no doubt, many mutually satisfying marriages which exist without the intimacy of deep friendship. These husbands and wives live together as practical business partners, cooperatively sharing the daily responsibilities while relating to each other with respect and care, but without much intellectual or emotional communication.

Some have other best friends with whom they can share with an openness and mutual understanding which seems impossible for them to experience with each other. Others appear to be able to live contentedly as private persons who have no in-depth friendship with anyone. When both husband and wife are happy with such an arrangement, we are grateful they found each other and applaud their marriage, but at the same time, confess that it would be difficult for either of us to find fulfillment in such an arrangement. There are "different strokes for different folks," and for us the sharing of intimate friendship is vital for our life together. If you are like us, we wish it also for you.

Pulling on the Beans

Most farmers are aware of the fact that "we can't make the beans grow by pulling on them." But many of us strain our marital friendship by trying to force change on one another. We may be able to forcibly change someone's behavior, but it's doubtful that pressure has much positive effect upon our attitudes or our long-range patterns of living. Coercion can often be counterproductive. When we sense that someone is out to change us, we tend to dig in our heels and become more stubborn than ever. On the other hand, when we sense that we are loved and accepted as we are, and are no longer threatened, we are free to let down our defenses and open the doors to change. Beyond that fact, no person is good enough to enslave another. *My* husband or wife is not *my* possession to control, but God's gift to love.

Living with such attitudes of acceptance is especially difficult for those who are idealists. It is wonderful to have high standards and noble goals, but if they are beyond human possibility, they can become tyrants that drive us to despair and our partners to depart. We all need what someone has called "the courage of imperfection" which recognizes that we are imperfect people living in an imperfect world.

Some people are so overwhelmed by the tyranny of an impossible ideal that they miss the happiness at hand because it does not compare with the imaginary joy of which they dream. Persons who flit from marriage to marriage like a bee from flower to flower are probably the victims of such a dream. They lack the frustration tolerance which is necessary to endure the pains of intimacy that are part of a relationship of depth. When the relationship begins to hurt, they fail to realize that the anguish may be the birth pangs of intimacy and so flee it like the plague. We hope you will have the wisdom and the courage to endure into the deeper meaning and the more profound happiness that lie beyond the pain. Having such endurance is a vital part of being a good friend.

"Be Good to Each Other"

Another essential ingredient of intimate friendship is in the attitude conveyed by the words, "Be good to each other." That advice, given not by the pastor at the wedding, but by a gas station attendant along the honeymoon route, made a deep impression on some friends of ours, and we have pondered it often.

Being good to each other, you will seek to give joy as well as to get it. You will try to do all you can to make your partner happy and will not be constantly preoccupied with "what's in it for me?" We will almost guarantee that when a husband and wife think almost exclusively in terms of what they should get from each other, they will both be miserable, but when they both think and act in terms of what they can give to each other, they will both be happy. Because sickness and misery can strike any life, we can't promise happiness to anyone, but we are sure that couples who do all they can to bring joy to each other are far happier than husbands and wives who seek only to get joy for themselves.

When Jesus said, "Whoever would save his life will lose it; and whoever loses his life for my sake, he will save it" (Luke 9:24), he stated a fact in life that is as true in marriage as everywhere else. When we lose ourselves in the abandonment of self-giving love, we discover a meaning and joy which is possible in no other way. We are apparently created to love and to be loved and to find our deepest joy in giving joy to others.

When a gift is given it needs to be received and acknowledged. Some of us have less trouble giving than receiving. We can be generous in sharing ourselves, but are too proud to let others give much to us. We probably fear that receiving something will obligate us to someone else and make us more dependent upon that person. But marriage is a relationship of interdependence and we do need each other. To be the proud giver without being a greateful receiver is to act out of a self-righteous superiority, which in the long run holds limited promise for mutual growth and fulfillment.

Mutual giving and receiving are part of the healthy rhythm of marriage. Mature partners are not afraid to ask gifts of each other, nor are they sparing in their expressions of gratitude. Words of appreciation are a vital part of the language of love. There are a hundred ways of saying "Thank you" and we do well to use them all, remembering that one of the best is simply to say it. To do so is not to be flatteringly phoney, but openly honest in response to another person's being good to us.

"I'm Sorry, Honey"

Being good to each other also means that we are good enough to admit that we aren't always good to each other. We believe the three most important three-word expressions in marriage are, first, "I love you," second, "Thank you, Honey," and third, "I'm sorry, Honey." It is not true in our experience that "love means never having to say 'I'm sorry.'"

There are certainly many nonverbal ways in which we confess our failures to one another and receive assurance of continued love, but there are also times to say it. Someone has pointed out that when husband and wife have an argument each may feel one hundred percent right and regard the other as one hundred percent wrong, but when one has the kindness and honesty to say to the other, "Honey, I think I was two percent wrong," the argument is often one hundred percent over.

It is as difficult to be one hundred percent right as it is to be one hundred percent wrong. When we are wrong it is right to confess it. One of us vividly remembers being corrected by an angry father who told his foolish child, "Don't be so damn stupid," and several hours later returned to ask the child's forgiveness. "You are not stupid," he said, "and I should not talk to you that way. Please forgive me." Neither such criticism nor such confession were the father's daily habit, but his action now stands in memory as a profound example of what it is to be a Christian example. Too often, whether in relation to parents and children or husbands and wives, we think of Christian example as saying, "Look at me, I'm perfect." Such arrogance is not Christian at all. True Christian example says, "I am far from perfect and need both the forgiveness of God and the forgiveness of those with whom I live."

We are often wrong in our attitudes even while being

right in our opinions. Our facts may be straight while our attitudes are crooked. Many a marriage has ended in misery because one or both partners were so stubbornly committed to being right that the whole relationship went wrong. We need to beware of the kind of arrogance which can result in winning many arguments while at some time destroying the marriage.

Confession is contagious. When we risk admitting our faults we free our partner to do the same. Admitting that I was "too hasty" opens the way for the other to be good to us. When one of us says, "I'm sorry I lost my temper this morning" the other can more easily reply, "I guess I had it coming for complaining so much before breakfast."

There is something humorous as well as pathetic in Jesus' story in Matthew 18:23-35 about the man who was forgiven a huge debt and then refused to forgive someone who owed him only a few dollars. Seeing ourselves in that parable can help us see the forgiveness we need to give in light of the forgiveness we need to receive and can help free us from conceited self-righteousness. Hopefully, we will have enough gratitude, self-awareness, and sense of humor to be both forgiven and forgiving. That spirit is an important part of our being good to each other.

Break the Vicious Circle

None of us lives with kindness all the time. We are greedy and grasping as well as giving and good. When we are hurt by our partner we are tempted to pull back our love and to retaliate in kind. Such retaliation may start a vicious circle of recrimination and revenge which must be broken if a relationship of giving and receiving love is to be restored.

Those of us who live with the promises of God's self-giving and forgiving love are enabled and encouraged to continue to be good and to do good to those who are often less than good to us. We are reminded that as we live by undeserved love we can hardly refuse to love someone who is sometimes less than loving toward us.

Specific steps toward breaking the vicious cycle are often difficult to take. We know of one wife—whose husband liked homemade bread—who vowed never to bake bread for him again. But after some days of reflection, she decided to be kind to him even if he were mean to her. She baked the bread, and the serving of it became a sign and sacrament of reconciliation that broke the vicious cycle and the wheel began to turn in the other direction. As meanness had followed meanness and hurt after hurt, a kind deed opened the way for kindness in return. Baking a few loaves of bread is not the solution to many marital problems, but when caught in a cycle of meanness one of us needs to do something that says, "Let's stop this nonsense and try to start a new cycle of kindness and love."

Be Angry!

Many people are surprised that the words, "Be angry" are in the Bible but here they are: "Be angry, but do not sin; do not let the sun go down on your anger . . ." (Ephesians 4:26). Those words come only a few verses before the passage that says, "Be kind to one another" (Ephesians 4:32) and they remind us to comment on the sometimes difficult problem of expressing our hostile feelings.

Being good to each other means sharing love and affection, and includes saying, "Thank you," "I love you," and "I'm sorry, Honey." But it also means having the honesty and courage to say, "I'm angry. . . !"

The people closest to us have the greatest potential for both helping and hurting us. Most of us can thank God for blessings received from our parents, but since none has had perfect parents we all have scars on our psyches as a result of their mistaken attitudes and actions. So also in marriage, we both help and hurt each other, and occasions of gratitude merge with times of anger.

Some of us "nice guys" may be reluctant to admit our angry feelings even to ourselves, but they will be expressed in one way or another. We may feel above making an emotional outburst or may think that "there's nothing to be done about it anyway, so why not forget it," but serious hostility is not disposed of so easily. One of us once visited a person in the hospital who was seriously ill with ulcers and related problems which are often psychosomatic in origin. He told of being utterly frustrated in trying to deal with the pastor of his church and confessed that "there isn't a thing I can do about it." But the fact is he did do something about it—he got sick! When negative feelings are not handled constructively they work on us like a corrosive acid poisoning both our bodies and our relationships.

"It Makes Me Mad . . .!"

It's fascinating and helpful to observe ways in which anger is expressed. Many persons retreat into silence, some scream and swear, rant or cry; others act out their anger by slamming doors or throwing something. Many of these patterns may have been caught from the families in which we grew up, and we may feel at home with our own way of reacting, even if we dislike it in others and are sometimes ashamed of it in ourselves.

But now what happens when, for example, a silent type gets married to a screamer, or a screamer to a thrower? At worst it may end the marriage in murder or divorce, but even at best there is a difficult adjustment to be made.

Talking with each other in calm moments about how we usually respond in times of hurt and resentment can be of great help in understanding each other. You may even discover that you can learn from each other. If you are silent, you may learn to let go and say something. If you have a short fuse and regret your explosions five minutes afterward, you can learn to count to one hundred instead of to ten.

In any case it is usually safe to confess *your* feelings without accusing each other. To say, "What you did makes me angry" is a factual description of how you feel. To call your partner a "stupid S.O.B." is, to say the least, a personal judgment of someone else. The former opens the gates of conversation; the latter slams the door in your spouse's face.

There are times when we are so out of touch with our own feelings that we are unaware of them ourselves. In such a case we may unwittingly express our anger in ways only indirectly related to the specific irritation. A wife resentful over her husband's infatuation with sports on TV may discover that she has a headache at bedtime. The husband, angry with his wife's bedtime headache, may forget to take out the garbage the next day.

We often catch ourselves behaving in such ways and continue to work at being more honest with each other. Although it's always tempting to express the anger indirectly or to go into a rage or retreat into a sulk, we've learned that it's usually wiser to say, "It makes me mad . . .!" and then take time to talk it through. We've also found it best to follow the biblical admonition, "Do not let the sun go down on your anger" by trying to verbalize our feelings as soon as possible following the offending incident. Doing this makes it easier for us to "be angry" without hurting ourselves or each other and eliminates those awful times of sulk and silence.

Who Decides What?

Like all married couples, we have had our difficulties in making decisions. Who decides what? What if we simply can't agree? Does the husband then get to make the final decision?

Some couples say that they try to decide things jointly but when they reach an impasse the husband, as "head of the house," chooses the course of action which the wife and children are duty-bound to obey. Thousands of families with wise and loving husbands live harmoniously with this arrangement. There is much to be said for it. When the wife is the submissive "heart of the house," willingly yielding responsibility for major decisions to a kind and sensitive husband who rules firmly and yet gently, order and harmony can be the result. The wife may feel relieved to be free from ultimate responsibility, and the husband's ego may be enhanced by his sense of authority and leadership.

Head and Heart?

But in spite of all that can be said for it, we don't like this "head and heart" arrangement. It suggests that the husband has all the brains and the wife all the emotions. We believe that the functions of "head" and "heart" should be shared by both husband and wife. In effect, there is, of course, much of such sharing in families which affirm the traditional head-heart roles. Some wives with subtle brilliance literally "rule the roost" while giving their husbands the appearance and sometimes the sense of doing so. But we think that it is wise to seek a better process of decision-making than the "when we can't agree it's up to him" arrangement.

Being male does not ensure the presence of either love or wisdom. Under "the husband rules" arrangement, wives with superior judgment are often condemned to live under the tyranny of arrogant folly. Even the husband with exceptional brilliance can be in error, and to be committed in advance to his every decision is a dangerous business. Beyond the wisdom of particular decisions, a wife who yields total responsibility for ultimate decision-making abdicates something essential to her full personhood and, at the same time, gives her husband responsibility he should not have to bear alone.

Other Arrangements

Another method of decision-making is to let the wife have the final say in everything. Needless to say, we don't like this either. The fact that many would ridicule such a matriarchal arrangement while applauding the patriarchal one is, in our opinion, one measure of the unconscious relegation of women to an inferior status in our society.

One step toward greater mutuality is for husbands and wives to yield freely authority for final decision-making *in certain areas* to each other. The husband with expertise in mechanical matters can, for example, choose the make of the family car, while the wife with greater sensitivity to color combinations is free to decorate the house. While this procedure seems to work well for some couples and is no doubt part of the unspoken contract of every harmonious marriage, we think it is at best a second-best arrangement. In actual practice it is often exceedingly one-sided. The husband may get to decide the place of residence, which is of course the area in which he can get the best job, and the wife can help pick the house and have almost full say in selecting the wallpaper. Or at the opposite extreme, the husband has full authority to decide the "big" issues concerning such things as national foreign policy, while the wife can decide the "little" things such as how they spend their money.

Not "Who's Right?" but "What's Right?"

The trouble with arrangements that give final authority to either husband or wife or try to divide the responsibility in some pre-agreed fashion is that both are in terms of "Who is right?" rather than "What is right?" In a relationship of mutual respect and love the important thing is not "Whose idea is it?" but "Is it the best idea?" To proceed in terms of "What's right?" without being able to fall back on either "It's up to me" or "It's up to you" can be frustrating, but as a democracy, though less efficient, is better for the country than dictatorship, we believe it is also better for family life.

Some Tests of Right and Wrong

There is no simple fail-safe method of always knowing what's right and what's wrong, but there are some "tests" to keep in mind as we ponder the significant choices of life. Here are a few of them, which we urge you to reflect upon and to discuss together:

—The law test: Is it (the contemplated action) in accordance with the Ten Commandments?

—The Golden Rule test: Is it in accordance with the Golden Rule, "Do unto others as you would have them do unto you?"

—The test of Jesus' new commandment: Is it in accord with Jesus' new commandment to "love one another as I have loved you?"

—The test of consequences: Is it hurtful or helpful to myself and others?

—The test of publicity: Is it something I'd be pleased to have everyone know about?

—The test of respected people: Is it something I'd like those whom I respect the most to know about?

—The test of universality: Would the world be better or worse if everyone were to act in the way I'm thinking of acting?

—The test of projected retrospect: Will I likely be pleased five/ten years from now to have done what I'm thinking of doing today?

—The test of Jesus' example: Is it something Jesus would do?

—The test of self-love: Does it express love of neighbor as of self? If I do this will I be caring as much for others as I care for myself?

__The test of conscience: Will I feel regret or gratitude after the deed is done or left undone?

It might be helpful for each of you to arrange this list in your order of importance and then talk with each other about why you have placed them as you did.

These "tests" relate most directly to decisions with moral implications, but some are also helpful in answering such questions as "Where should we live?" or "What kind of car should we buy?" which are less directly ethical in nature.

To illustrate the way in which these "tests" work out in practice, think of the following examples of the application of the test of projected retrospect.

Suppose that husband or wife while away at a convention is tempted toward a short-term affair which could probably be kept secret. There seems little doubt that it would add fun and excitement to an otherwise dull and dreary week. But at the same time the thought of either having to live with this secret for the rest of one's life or else having to tell it to a certain displeasure and possible retaliation of a spouse is enough to tip the scales in favor of resisting the temptation. From the perspective of projected retrospect, it is clear that long-term fulfillment is more important than a short-term fling.

Or suppose a couple is trying to decide whether to move to another city where the husband is offered a better job or to stay put for another year so that the wife can complete additional academic work which is essential to further development of her career. There is no doubt that they would be better off financially for the next few years if they were to move, and the wife is sometimes sick of school and on bad days thinks it might be nice to give up the career, settle down, and raise a family. But at the same time as they imagine themselves ten years down the road looking back at this decision, they are both certain they would live to regret it and, therefore, decide that long-term fulfillment requires a decision to stay.

In terms of the broad lines of our most important decisions and total style of life, it is wise occasionally to project ourselves to the end of life and to ask how our present way of living looks from that perspective. We may then decide that the rat race really isn't worth it or that it is better to spend our money for the down payment on a home or for regular weekends away together than to buy a new luxury car.

The Options Are Open

The "What's right?" approach does not impose pre-assumed solutions on any problem. Because the husband is offered more money at a new position in a different city, it is not taken for granted that the couple will automatically pack up and move. More money is only one factor in the decision. The wife's employment, relationships with friends, educational and cultural opportunities for all the family, and many other factors may be of equal or far greater significance—and it is necessary to weigh them all in attempting to decide the best course of action.

When operating with the "What's right?" procedure, some decisions will be easy. The answer will often seem obvious and mutual agreement will be almost instantaneous. But sometimes much study and discussion will be necessary before a consensus is reached, and on occasion husband and wife will arrive at diametrically opposed conclusions. The husband may be convinced that the offered promotion is the "chance of a lifetime" and that he would be crazy to turn it down. The wife may feel that "a move to that city will make it impossible for me to complete my education and will destroy my lifelong dream of a personal career."

What should they do? We don't know but we don't think either should automatically give in to the authority or pressure of the other. Have they fully explored all the possibilities? Are they objective about the facts of the matter? Is it really impossible for the wife to complete her education in the other city? Is his job offer really "the chance of a lifetime?" For mutual personal fulfillment, are they able to endure being apart for awhile? If one must sacrifice, for whom is the sacrifice the less severe? To keep the decision focused on "What's the best course of action?" it may be helpful to bring in an objective third person or outside couple, not to make the decision, but to help clarify the issues and weigh the alternatives.

Through this process one course of action will usually emerge as being at least slightly preferable to the others, and both can agree that this, while painful, is best. Both will feel the pain and neither will be only capitulating to or "lording" it over the other. But if, after careful study and objective conversation, he still says, "I'm going to move and take the job," while she maintains, "I'm going to stay and pursue my career," they have obviously agreed to separate temporarily at least, and must next decide what this means for their marriage. If the choice of temporary separation reflects the value each places on career fulfillment and is not just a power play to coerce the other, it may be a responsible, proper decision. To say this is not to degrade the value of the relationship but only to face the fact that marriage is based upon mutual respect and love and that it gives neither husband nor wife the right to coerce or enslave the other.

Times to Give In

There are certainly times when one will choose to give in to the other even when convinced that he or she is wrong.

None of us is perfectly reasonable, and we all have a capacity for stubbornness. Given this fact we need to see every specific issue in light of the worth of the total relationship. If the wife is convinced that the family should go out for supper and the husband, seeing the refrigerator full of left-overs, is sure that dinner out is a wasteful extravagance, it may be wise for one to yield quickly and quietly to the other without going to war over it. If the husband loves his wife and is financially able to do so, her needs and desires will mean more to him than the cost of the dinner. If the wife knows the dinner out will necessitate dropping plans for a concert her husband deeply desires to hear, she will get busy warming up the left-overs.

Such mutual consideration is part of the compromising that enables persons in love to live together harmoniously across the years. To give in under pressure alone may be a sign of weakness, but to give in out of love and wisdom is a mark of strength. Persons secure in themselves don't need to be right on every issue, nor do they stubbornly insist on everything always going their way. "Love does not insist on it's own way" (1 Corinthians 13:5) but gives consideration to the needs and feelings of others. Such love gives people room to make their own mistakes and to act in ways which are prompted more by emotional desire than by rational thought. This does not mean love itself is irrational but that it sees the emotional needs of life to be of great importance and that they must be given at least equal consideration alongside the rational factors. For example, to squelch a partner's need for creative, cultural, or recreational expression because "it's more rational to invest the money in the stock market" may in the long run be as foolish as it is cruel.

Acting with loving consideration for another person's feelings does not mean to be a puppet at the end of that person's strings nor a doormat over which everyone else is welcome to walk. Every virtue needs to be balanced by its opposite virtue. Unselfish concern for other persons needs to be balanced by a proper respect for oneself. Spouses who always give in out of love may build a reservoir of resentment which may eventually be more destructive to the marriage than the momentary conflict that comes from refusal to yield to his or her every whim. So even as we stress that there are times to give in, we also assert that there are times to stand firm. One of the true marks of maturity is to have the love and wisdom to know the one from the other. We have no magic means of gaining that knowledge, but are sure that when commitment to "What's right?" rather than "Who's right?" is combined with sincere respect for one's own and for each other's personal needs, a couple have come a long way toward the maturity in which wisdom and love are the dominant factors in decision-making.

Look for Specific Solutions

One thing we have learned through frequently painful experience is that it is usually better to seek a specific solution to the problem at hand, rather than gripe about each other's faults. If the husband persists in leaving his dirty socks on the bedroom floor, it can be an occasion to remind him, "You are the sloppiest man on earth." To really do such fault-finding right, the wife will be sure to say, "Your mother picked up after you for years and spoiled you rotten, so it's no wonder you never grew up." Such comments will likely do nothing either to improve the marriage or to move the socks.

Many wives, seeing the socks, and remembering that they have some habits that are irritating to their husbands, will solve the problem by simply picking them up themselves.

Others may put a cardboard "socks box" in the closet and suggest that the husband, who has always been a hotshot basketball player, prove his skill by tossing his socks into it. He may reply, "I'll do that if you'll stop leaving all your junk on the bathroom sink." Such willingness to work out an "I'll do something for you if you do something for me" arrangement is a necessary part of civilized living together.

One specific thing each partner can do for the other is to contract to begin each day with courtesy. We can't become perpetually kind by willing to be so, but most of us can manage fifteen or twenty minutes in the morning. Being good to each other, or at least refraining from being unkind, during those morning minutes, even when we feel sleepy and irritable, can help set the stage for a better day for everyone involved. As a general rule, it is unwise to make major decisions in a state of emotional distress and, unless you are both serene and happy in the morning, the time between bed and departure for work is usually better spent in positive anticipation of the possibilities of the day than in bickering over the problems of the past or present.

Postponement of discussion of touchy subjects can, of course, lead to the avoidance of such conversation altogether. If we are to set times when we will not talk about certain things, we may need to be equally firm in contracting for specific occasions when we promise to really hear each other out. Instead of doing the slow burn for days or weeks because he or she "never brings it up" or "obviously doesn't want to talk about it," the silence is better broken by saying, "I need to talk with you" and then either proceeding or setting a time to do so.

There are, of course, people who have such great difficulty in firmly deciding anything that they usually opt for almost perpetual indecision. Some seem to live in the hope that problems will go away or that something will happen to make it unnecessary to deal with them. Others assume the role of a child and look to the father-husband or mother-wife to make the decisions and then complain that their partners are running their lives.

To decide to do nothing is, in effect, to choose to let things go on as they are. While it is sometimes wise to postpone making a decision, this kind of indecision is often the worst decision of all. Each of us needs to be occasionally reminded that we live in a real world where hard decisions must be made and that we cannot live together in marriage as equally responsible adults while expecting the other, or permitting ourselves, to make all the decisions.

When Habits Clash

The principle of "look for a specific solution" is especially helpful in dealing with the adjustments related to different styles of living. A husband, for example, may be extremely neat and orderly. He can't stand living with mess and disorder. Just walking into a room with newspapers and magazines haphazardly tossed on the furniture or toys strewn on the floor makes him uncomfortable. His wife, on the other hand, is actually a little ill at ease when everything is properly in place and doesn't even notice the so-called mess he complains about. She likes the house to look "lived in" and picking up once a week or before company comes is sufficient for her.

To avoid endless frustration and bickering, some mutual accommodation is obviously necessary. Respectfully recognizing their differing attitudes toward neatness to be part of individual personality makeup, rather than convictions consciously chosen to "bug each other," they are free to concentrate on solving the problem itself. Their solution may be that the husband will do the vacuuming once a week if the wife will pick up the newspapers before supper

41

and have the children return the toys to the toy box before going to bed.

Or suppose the husband is a night owl, while his wife likes to go to bed with the chickens. By ten P.M. his head is alive with hopes of zestful romance and she is ready to collapse. If he yields to her suggestion, "Let's wait till morning," the situation may then be reversed. Rested and refreshed, the wife is ready for an exciting start to the new day, but now he is so "conked out" it is difficult to get him up in time for work, to say nothing of anything else.

It takes creativity, love, and patience to reach a mutually satisfying accommodation in such circumstances. Hopefully, there is some time during the day or night when they are both together and awake at the same time. When such times are limited, care must be taken that these precious moments to be preserved as islands of intimacy in all its dimensions rather than wasted through preoccupation with details of traditional routine. Right after dinner may be the usual time to wash the dishes, but this could be done later by the night-owl husband or the next morning by the early-bird wife so that they could have freedom for a couple of hours of early evening intimacy, some of which could be enjoyed with the door locked and the phone off the hook.

Alone Together

When children are growing up, the responsibilities and distractions of parenthood often conflict with the total intimacy needs of marriage. The fun time after supper often has to give way to the needs of a crying child. But don't let this cause you to give up on efforts to find times and places to be husband and wife as well as father and mother. Just because something is difficult doesn't make it impossible. If children come to so dominate the home scene that little intimacy is possible, arrangements may need to be made to get away for regular weekends together. Some couples have a standing arrangement to exchange caring for each other's children a weekend a month so that each will have at least that much time alone together.

As we think of our being both spouses and parents, we are reminded that some people become so possessed by their roles as father and mother that they cease to speak to each other as persons, but rather address each other as parents. We realize that in speaking with a child it is natural to say, "Mother wants to see you" or "Daddy would like you to help him," but urge you to call each other by your own names, rather than start addressing each other as "Mother" and "Father." Be persons and not just roles to one another.

When a couple live with in-laws or have other semi-public housing arrangements, the preservation of privacy is especially difficult. Such arrangements may be temporarily necessary, but we believe every couple should endeavor to have their own home or apartment. When there are children, a lock on the bedroom door is a minimum necessity, and a room arrangement in which the couple is free from fears of being overheard is highly desirable. In our opinion, most homebuilders have given too little attention to this need. If planned into the home, privacy can be economically provided. Yet, because many are apparently either thoughtless or too embarrassed to talk about it, homes continue to be built without adequate provision for it.

Speaking of Sex . . .

We believe that, at best, sexual relations can be one of the most significant "sacraments" of married love. There are certainly many other "sacramental" moments in marriage—mealtimes, playtimes, times of laughter, tearful times, times shared with close friends, times for going on a date together—but sexual relations are a special means of saying, "I love you" and "I want you to love me," which can renew the relationship and give deep personal satisfaction to both partners. In our opinion, sex is the wonderful gift of a loving God who has endowed us with this capacity and desire not only, or even primarily, for the creation of children, but for our mutual joy.

In spite of (or is it sometimes because of?) all that has been printed and pictured about sex in recent years, misunderstandings still seem to abound. Many, for example, apparently think that sex appeal is a physical aspect that can be measured with a tape measure. While appreciating the beauty of a shapely lady or the build of an athletic man, we are convinced that the sexiest part of our bodies is above the neck. The eyes—the voice—the facial expression—the thoughts—the words—these above all are the marks of a "sexy" man or woman. Other physical attributes, of course, contribute or detract, and we should do all that we can to maintain our physical health and appearance, but in this regard they are usually of secondary importance. A sexy mind is more important than a sexy body. Because many fail to realize this fact, they are unnecessarily depressed over self-diagnosed lack of attractiveness, while others are deluded into thinking a well-endowed body alone gives them special sex appeal. Sex appeal, sexual ability, and sexual satisfaction have only limited relation to physical factors. Learning this fact can give some people a new lease on sexual life.

As in other areas of married life, our best word on your sexual relationship may be simply to urge you again to "Be good to each other." Treat each other with tenderness and affection. Here, as everywhere, do what you can to give happiness, pleasure, and joy to each other. There will be times when you will not be particularly interested in the sexual invitations of the other, but you will not harshly push each other aside. In love you will sometimes permit what you did not desire and often be surprised by joy in doing so. At other times, the same love will restrain your desire so that you will not attempt to coerce or ridicule your partner.

Bed and Breakfast

Someone has said, "What happens at bedtime is often determined by how a husband and wife treat each other at breakfast." This is not to suggest a calculated breakfast ritual intended to pay off later, but is, rather, to emphasize the fact that our specific sexual experiences are always related to all the other dimensions of our total relationship. Some people who treat their spouses with indifference and disrespect all day wonder why their sexual overtures are rejected at bedtime. It would actually be surprising to be otherwise. How can persons whose minds are filled with bitterness and resentment freely and fully give their bodies to each other in the abandonment of sexual love.

This is not to suggest that sexual overtures are always out of place when resentments exist. The prelude to sexual relations in these circumstances can include conversation that bridges the chasm of estrangement and opens the way to a sexually sacramental reunion of minds and hearts as well as bodies.

As what happens at breakfast influences what happens at bedtime, so also what happens at bedtime, or before breakfast in bed, influences what happens at breakfast and through the rest of the day. Our lives are a complex tapestry woven of many strands intertwined together. Each aspect of life affects all the others. Trouble with in-laws can, for example, disrupt an otherwise beautiful sexual relationship, and persistent sexual frustration can result in resentments which are expressed in a big blowup over a coming visit from in-laws. Recognizing the interplay of all these factors helps us sort things out so that we can come to terms with our true difficulties rather than dealing only with symptoms.

It's Not Always the Same

We also think it's important to realize that the experience of sexual relations is not always the same. Sometimes it's like having a seven-course candlelight dinner. At other times it's more like going to McDonald's for a hamburger. But what's so bad about that? As we can enjoy and be refreshed by both McDonald's and the finest restaurant, we can also enjoy and be enriched by a great variety of sexual experiences. Remembering this can help free a couple from unnecessary and destructive preoccupation with performance and from obsessive attempts to achieve supreme ecstasy in every encounter. Sexual relations can be beautiful in moods of play and fun and in more serene times of tender love, but they are seldom lovely when regarded as work, a contest, or a competitive sport. To think in terms of "scoring" or "keeping score" is destructive to a sexual relationship.

Don't Try So Hard

From what we hear of problems in this department, many couples are trying too hard. There are many things we can't do by trying. Trying hard to get aroused or to have an ultimate sexual experience is like trying to go to sleep. The more you try the worse it is. Wouldn't it often be better for the insomniac to try to stay awake and for the unresponsive to try not to get turned on? At least, we seem to sleep best and respond most naturally when no one, including ourselves, is telling us we have to do so. A couple's bedroom should be a place of rest and refreshment, free from demands, where they can relax and enjoy being together. In sexual relations as everywhere else, we are invited to live "by grace." We are to trust more than try, being open to receive gifts beyond our achieving. Grace doesn't demand anything; it doesn't say, "You must do this or that," but rather, "This is my gift to you." Sexual response is not something we achieve by our own effort. It is a gift of love received from our lover. When we look to ourselves and think of what we ought to do or feel, our attention is distracted away from the very stimulation that can produce the responses we may be so desperately seeking. We find the most fulfillment when we approach our sexual experiences without demanding anything of ourselves or each other. We don't even need to feel obligated to have sexual relations. Times of returning to the romantic patterns of courtship without intercourse can be meaningful for all of us. Don't miss the joy of just being close and tender with each other.

Some men seem to need assurance that tenderness is a masculine emotion, when as a matter of fact, it takes a real man to be tender and affectionate. There are apparently some women who love to be overwhelmed by brute force, but as we understand it, the famous lovers of history are not the caveman types, but are, rather, those who know how to be sincerely kind and considerate. When we act that way we are expressing an honest concern for someone else. Sexual love is more than an unselfish caring for another person, but it is never complete without it. In your sexual encounters, as in hundreds of other ways, we hope you will both be strong enough to be tender and affectionate with each other.

Laugh at Yourselves

Part of what is involved here is a sense of humor. We need to laugh at ourselves and to chuckle together over our blunders and clumsiness. This is not to endorse ridicule or cynical, sarcastic humor which makes fun of another person. That, too, can be disastrous to a sexual relationship. But we should not take ourselves too seriously. With good humor we can be free and playful without fear of being insulted or put down.

We don't recommend that you take a copy of the latest How-to-do-it book along on your honeymoon. Save that for later—maybe even five, ten, twenty years later. Do your own exploring and experimenting. We think that making your own discoveries will be more interesting and exciting. As you are able to leave your inhibitions behind, lovingly and playfully explore the dimensions of sexual love. As you have life and health, you will likely have many years for such exploration. You don't need to try everything the first week you are married. Take time to learn what pleases each other.

Recently we heard a reportedly old illustration concerning the frequency of sexual relations in marriage. As this story goes, a supposedly wise father tells his son, soon to be married, that if he puts a bean in a jar for each time he and his wife have intercourse during their first year of marriage and then after the first year, removes a bean for each sexual encounter, the jar will never be empty. We emphatically disagree. Without having taken any scientific surveys on the subject, we expect that most healthy couples will empty the jar in only slightly more time then it took them to fill it, and that there will be no dramatic decrease in the frequency of sexual relations at any point in their marriage. That there will be a gradual lessening is to be expected, but this decrease in quantity may be more than compensated for by an increase in quality. As with other great arts, the beauty of sexual relations can be increased with understanding, love, and much practice.

Speaking of such a lifelong honeymoon prompts us to add a word concerning the specific honeymoon that usually follows the wedding. Those days were wonderful for us, but we certainly don't regard them as "the best time of our lives." We have also learned from a number of couples that there are those for whom they are not wonderful at all.

There are probably few institutions so overloaded with heavy expectations as the honeymoon in particular and both sex and marriage in general. It is especially here that patience, long-term perspective, and a sense of humor become of tremendous importance.

Regarding honeymoon trips, we urge that couples not attempt to see the whole world, but rather, plan for lots of leisure to just enjoy being together. On the other hand, doing nothing but being together can also be a bit much, so seeing a little of the world might well be in order.

If You Have Problems

We don't anticipate that you'll have any serious problems in your sexual relationship and don't want you to worry about having them. We are grateful for having been so naïve when we got married that we didn't even know what the potential problems might be. If you have read some of the literature that now abounds on this subject, we urge you to forget it. Be good to each other, laugh at your blunders, and ninety-nine percent of the problems will solve themselves.

But if there are difficulties in this area, or in any other, which persist and threaten your personal fulfillment or continued relationship, don't just endure them in resentful silence. Even if it is painful to do so, share your concerns with each other; and if this is not sufficient to resolve the difficulty, seek a counselor who can often provide helpful information and insight. We should treat ourselves and our marriages at least as well as we treat our cars. None of us would let a new car with a mechanical problem sit at the curb for six months without doing anything to repair it. Yet many live for years with personal and marital problems and do nothing to correct them. Each new day is full of potential for renewal of life, and we sometimes need a bit of outside help to discover and experience it. Part of your marriage commitment might be spelled out in a specific contract in which you agree to seek help on those problems you are unable to resolve by yourselves. If a marriage is going to work, both husband and wife have to work at it. One spouse can kill a marriage but it takes two to keep it alive and healthy.

Getting Out of Old Ruts

Someone has described a rut as "a grave with the ends knocked out," and there can be times in marriage when we seem to be living in that kind of rut. There are no special problems, no crisis over which to contemplate divorce or murder, but we feel the old spark is gone. Everything is so daily. We are only going through the motions. When these times come we are up against something which may be the number one enemy of joyful marriage, and its name is not "crisis" or "conflict" but boredom.

We can often manage the major crisis situations quite well. When illness strikes or financial disaster threatens, we rise to the challenge and work together with a sense of meaning and purpose. In those circumstances our situation may be like that of a person who reported that while huddled in a London bomb shelter during World War II, he suddenly realized, "I have very few problems." When survival is at stake, most of our more petty problems suddenly disappear from sight. But when we resume the regular routine, they usually reappear, though, hopefully, in a bit better perspective, and we must again deal with them. Among the most difficult of these is the sometimes deadly effect of the routine itself.

Battles with Boredom

The problem of boredom is especially difficult when it afflicts only one partner. She is perfectly content and considers the marriage the most satisfying experience of her life, while he feels that life together is dull as dust. Or he may be the one who can't believe his wife is bored with a relationship that seems to him such a good marriage. In the extremes of these differences of feeling, we encounter the exceedingly painful situation in which one says, "I'm sorry, but I can't stand to live with you any longer," while the other says, "I love and need you so much, I am not sure that I can live without you."

When boredom is involved the intense feelings fortunately don't develop overnight, and there are things we can do to deal with them. Some are simple but significant, such as giving each other freedom to plan things we do together. When one is bored, it is usually because that person feels stifled and unfulfilled. We seem to be trapped with no way out. Facing that fact and literally looking together for ways to get out of the old ruts, and then caring enough to follow through on them, is often enough to be the start of a new lease on life.

In Each Other's Shoes

But the only way this can happen is for each of us to practice the ancient but difficult art of standing in each other's shoes. He may feel that going out for dinner is a waste of time and money and she may think that his idea of having some clean fun by taking a shower together is downright silly. But if they really care for each other and are concerned with each other's happiness and fulfillment, they will not lightly brush such suggestions aside. We are not advocates of exorbitant waste, nor of continually silly behavior, but there are times when a little wastefulness and some silly abandonment really brighten the day and add zest to living. Jesus praised the woman who wasted costly ointment in an expression of lavish love (Matthew 26:6-13). His act invites us to be more liberated and at least a little lavish in our expression of love to one another.

On a more profound and serious level, boredom probably reflects unfulfilled expectations of the marriage and of each other. If these expectations are unrealistically excessive and would be unfulfilled in any marriage with any person, we need to come to terms with them. It may be that we are not so much bored with the marriage as with life itself, and especially with ourselves, and are more in need of personal renewal than of a new spouse. When this seems to be true, it is time for honest self-examination of our basic values and goals in life, and an occasion to seek new avenues of personal, vocational, and spiritual fulfillment.

When All Else Fails

What if the expectations were realistic but are being increasingly unfulfilled? Is all lost and hopeless or can the spirit of courtship be revived? The fact that the relationship was once exciting enough to lead to marriage holds promise that it can be so again. To face and confess feelings of disappointment costs some pride and risks resentment, but to do so is another essential part of the painful price of intimacy. You may discover that your apparently contented partner isn't so content after all, and that you are both open to deeper dimensions of sharing which can lead out of boredom into meaning and joy. If you can't communicate these feelings alone together, the presence of an understanding counselor may help you share them and explore possibilities for new beginnings.

If through all this everything fails and you come to the honest and realistic conclusion that the marriage is dead, there may be no alternative in love or wisdom but to have a funeral for it. We are not advocates of separation and divorce, but are realistic enough to acknowledge that marriages which are mutually destructive of husbands and wives, and which seem devoid of possibil. for healing, are better ended then prolonged. But such a sion should not be made lightly or in a fit of angry passion. Persons contemplating divorce face an awesome decision and need to ask themselves sincerely, "Is this what I really want?" "Will this solve my problems?" "Is there nothing further we can do to renew our relationship?"

Some divorces lead to positive new beginnings for everyone involved, but in others people aln. st literally go "from the frying pan into the fire." Perhap. seems out of place to think of these things in a letter lik his, but in a society in which thousands of marriages n divorce, honest realism seems to demand it. Putt divorce into perspective now may help to avoid the nec ty of thinking of it later.

Concerns from
Kids to Kinfolk

That a couple would have children if physically possible was until recently taken for granted. The fact that this can no longer be assumed seems to us a positive sign of more responsible parenthood. We love our children and thank God for them and, at the same time, believe that parenthood should be freely chosen and properly planned for.

There are some whose only family planning is that "We will have as many children as God gives us." To us this seems as irresponsible as for a rabbit raiser to say, "I will raise as many rabbits as God gives me," without giving adequate consideration to how he will feed and care for them. God gives us more than sexual desire and the physical potential for parenthood; he also gives us brains and the responsibility to use them as wise stewards of all his gifts. As we rightly thank God for our sexual powers, we also thank him for ways of being more responsible in their use. Specifically this can mean that even as a couple thank God for the joy and pleasure of sexual relations, they also say, "Praise the Lord" for the pills or other means of contraception which give them the freedom to share their love sexually without fear of unwanted pregnancy. The possibility of unhealthy side effects from methods of birth control must, of course, be considered, and a medical doctor is best qualified to advise on these matters, but morally speaking, we believe their use to be a blessing for which we thank God and not a sin we are called to confess.

Do not take chances, thinking, "We can always have an abortion." In the first place, "we" don't have an abortion, the wife does—and it is never a pleasant experience. A wise wife and loving husband will never select abortion as their method of birth control. Beyond such consideration, we must confess that we consider abortion at best a tragic necessity. Our experience of having lost our first baby girl, who was born during the fifth month of pregnancy and lived only an hour, has no doubt deeply influenced our belief and feeling in this regard. The thought of deliberately ending the life of an unborn child is terribly disturbing to us and underscores our urging responsible contraception so that it will never be necessary to consider an abortion.

If it is responsible for some couples to decide to have no children, is it also proper for others to have more than two or three? We think you must make your own decision in light of your personal circumstances seen within the wider context of global population concerns. For an outside authority to decide arbitrarily that any particular couple must either limit or increase their number of children seems to us a denial of personal responsibility and freedom. The population-food crisis may become so severe that this freedom will be no longer possible, but we are hopeful that worldwide assumption of personal and social responsibility will make such legalistic birth regulation unnecessary.

Then There Is Money

There is an old saying, "It's no sin to be poor but it's a terrible inconvenience"—and that's a fact! Is it also true, as

D. H. Lawrence is reported to have said, that "A woman who is in love with a man will sleep on a board"? Will a man in love with a woman be as content with as little? Just how important is money in a marital relationship?

It seems to depend on the couple. If one or both are more in love with money and things than with each other, a situation of rivalry can occur, threatening the marriage in a way similar to the presence of an outside lover. The husband who cares more for his car than for his wife, and the wife who regards her house as a greater treasure than her husband, are in a shaky marital situation.

In our experience, the quality of our relationship has been much more important than the amount of money in the bank. We come from families of limited means, simple tastes, and frugal habits and have at the same time been spared extreme poverty. We have also had many rich educational and cultural opportunities. We can't say how our marriage would have thrived under adverse conditions but are sure that if either or both of us were to live in ways which kept us on the verge of bankruptcy, it would certainly be extremely hurtful to our relationship.

Our money problems have been more with management than amount. We share the same checking account and sometimes get into trouble by failing to record all the checks. There have occasionally been intense differences over specific spending decisions, with one of us considering a certain expenditure an urgent necessity, while the other sees it as a wasteful luxury or believes the money would be better used for something else—but we have thus far been able to arrive at mutually acceptable agreements or compromises.

Keeping our financial records has been mainly a feminine responsibility, but we think that this is entirely a matter of personal agreement, ability, and interest and can as well be reversed. Most couples are wise to plan a budget together with equal regard for the needs and desires of each partner.

Both should have some freedom to make individual purchases, but major items should be mutually decided upon. If you have limited experience with family budgeting, it may be wise to sit down with someone who can help establish a model procedure to guide you.

Discipline is required in order to escape the temptation to fritter away our money on things that have no significant or lasting value. If we want to be rich it seems best to become so not by securing everything we selfishly want, but by reducing our wants to our needs. When we have all we need, what more do we need?

Money has been described as "our time and talent in portable form." Our money is an extension of ourselves. We use it most wisely when we spend it for our good and the good of others. One millionaire said, "I never had any fun with my money until I began to do good with it." His experience again witnesses to the fact that we find fulfillment in life when we give ourselves away in love to others. In marriage, as in other human relationships, it is extremely doubtful that we can long enjoy luxuries for ourselves while we refuse to provide necessities for others. Be honest in sharing your true needs with each other and try your best to put first things first. With regard to spending both money and time, we need to distinguish between the "musts" and the "maybes" in life. When there is a choice to be made, the rent must be paid and the sailboat will have to wait.

What about Work?

During our twenty years together we have experienced three of the most common marital work arrangements: only the wife working while the husband completed school; only the husband working while the wife was busy with babies, homemaking, and completing additional education; and both husband and wife working full time. Each stage has had its special joys and problems, but all things considered, we would do it that way again. We are intrigued, however, by some of the new arrangements, such as husband and wife each working half time, and hope that the business world will become increasingly open to this possibility so that couples will have more opportunity to share their lives with each other and with their children.

When the wife is working outside the home, or has a virtually full-time job in caring for young children, the husband will see that sharing household duties is not doing her a favor, but part of his own responsibility. In this situation the specific housework assumed by each partner will depend upon personal interest and abilities. Talk it out and divide the work as fairly as you can. A clear understanding of mutually accepted responsibilities helps to avoid repeated resentment and continual conflict. Don't just nag at each other about what's not being done. Face the tasks at hand and work out specific contracts for their completion. Then assume your personal responsibilities to fulfill these commitments to each other as you would if they were made with someone else. If it turns out that this is impossible to do, renegotiate the contract. Don't let it die by default. If one arrangement is bad, work toward another that is better.

Times to Play

We once heard a lecture for engaged and married couples entitled, "Married for Keeps" and subtitled, "Facts for Fumblers Frankly Faced." One specific suggestion made by the speaker was that wives and husbands occasionally play a game of tiddly-winks on the living room rug before going to bed. The purpose of this suggestion was to get couples into a playful mood as a prelude to what might happen in bed. Whatever its significance for bedtime, that advice has great importance for the rest of the marriage.

Without some kind of playful renewal, marriage can settle into a routine of working, eating, sleeping, and even making love that can become dull and lifeless. There is a child within each of us who wants to sing, dance, and play. This child needs room to run, but some marriages are so grim and serious that the poor child within is nearly stifled to death. Our hearts go out to such couples, wishing that somehow they might feel once more the joy of running barefoot in the sand and sense again the thrill of playful, tender love. There are heavy responsibilities in life, and serious concerns demand our time and attention. But we can't live well under perpetual pressure and, therefore, need frequent occasions of getting-away-from-it-all to be renewed in our persons and in our relationship. Jesus took time to see the flowers and be apart in a quiet place. If we get busier than he was, we are likely too busy for either our good or the good of others.

Having Friends

We especially enjoy getting together with other couples and have always been grateful that we are enough alike to appreciate each other's friends. It has often been true that just spending an evening visiting or going to a movie with another couple has helped to renew us personally and to refresh our relationship with each other.

Others tell of special problems in this regard. One may be so attached to old friends that the other becomes jealous and resentful, or both may seek fulfillment so completely in each other that they cut themselves off from others. We hope that you will be able to share old friends together and, at the same time, be open to new relationships. Don't just "stew in your own juice." Invite others to share their venture of life with you and be open to share yours with them. Your doing so can be therapeutic and life-fulfilling for everyone involved.

Each of us also has a number of friends and co-workers with whom we share certain concerns which are not of interest to each other. Being reasonably secure in our relationship, these have never been a threat to us. They are, rather, another reminder that it is not possible for us to be everything, or everyone, to each other and that we should, therefore, not attempt to be so. Even as we remain husbands and wives after becoming fathers and mothers, we also remain persons after becoming husbands and wives and need freedom for nonromantic friendships which enable personal fulfillment beyond the gifts we can give each other.

Being Alone

Even as we stress the importance of having mutual and personal friends, a word needs to be said about also giving each other freedom to be alone. In the total rhythm of life, times of solitude and socializing alternate with one another. The fact that each of you will continue to desire to do some things by yourself rather than together is not the sure sign of a bad marriage. Just as we need each other, we also need times and places to be alone with our own thoughts and to pursue our personal interests. A husband who feels rejected because his wife would rather read a book than spend the evening with him watching TV or the wife who thinks her husband is short on love because he prefers to work in the shop or garden than accompany her shopping, may need to ask if they are becoming excessively possessive of each other.

Refusing to watch TV together or retreating to the shop may be signs of rejection, but these may just as likely be signs of legitimate longings for personal fulfillment which are properly fulfilled alone.

Getting Along with In-laws

Persons soon to be married sometimes reply to inquiries about how they expect to get along with in-laws by saying, "I'm not marrying his or her family, I'm marrying him or her." While literally true, such thinking does not represent the total truth. For better or worse, we marry into each other's families and, while in-law jokes abound, this fact is sometimes no joke. When problems arise, the difficulties seem to come especially from two sources and often from both at the same time: on the one hand, from the attitudes and actions of anxious overprotective parents and, on the other, from the attitudes and actions of immature, insensitive, defensive children.

As parents, we need to give our children freedom to make their own mistakes and, at the same time, to be available for support and guidance as needed and wanted. Mature children will realize that this is extremely difficult to do. For parents to see someone they love following a road they are convinced leads to misery and regret and to be told to "mind your own business" is exceedingly painful.

One of the most common faults of parents, and perhaps also of husbands and wives, arises from failure to realize that suggestions often imply criticism. When we frequently suggest, "Why don't you do it this way?" we may be heard as saying, "I think you are too stupid to know how to do anything right." Then, surprised that our kind and innocent suggestions are met with resistance and hostility, we defend ourselves by saying, "I am only trying to be help-ful," which may be heard as "I am strong, wise, and helpful; you are weak, foolish, and much in need of my help."

The ability to give and receive suggestions depends largely on whether it is within an essentially adult-adult rather than parent-child relationship. Mature parents rec-ognize that suggestions imply criticism and are sparing in making them, preferring, if anything, to offer some tentative alternatives for action and leaving the decisions to those who must live with them. Mature children also recognize that there are many ways in which they need to learn and be helped and are not too proud to receive an idea or a gift from parents. Immature wives and husbands, who are insecure in the newly won freedom of adulthood, find it especially difficult to accept advice or counsel from their parents. Some are so defensive that they are offended by the most wise and helpful suggestions and will, if anything, do the opposite, even to their own hurt, just to prove their independence.

We hope that you are mature enough to listen to advice from others, including your parents, to weigh it carefully, and then do what seems best to you. Do not let any outside person, be it parent or peer, run your lives. Remember again, it is not a question of "Who's right?" but of "What's right?" When a parent gives you an excellent idea, be mature enough to take it, but if it's a lousy idea, be smart enough and strong enough to reject it firmly and kindly.

Since parents are usually more willing to accept opinions from their own offspring than from a son-in-law or a daughter-in-law, we suggest that if serious conflicts arise you should each take the central role in dealing with your own parents. It takes skill and patience to be firm in rejecting a parental viewpoint without rejecting them as persons. When they see that you appreciate their concern and respect their counsel, even when rejecting it, they will likely grow in ability to let you make your own decisions.

If you have come through some painful cross-generational tension during adolescence, you may be surprised to begin to enjoy your parents' presence and to discover that they seem, for the first time in years, to be doing the same. You have moved out of the parent-child situation into a new relationship of adult-adult encounter in which you meet as equals. While this shift is never total, it can be the basis of mutual understanding and joy for both generations.

As you marry into each other's families, you also marry the family within each other. Even if you are thousands of miles away from your nearest relatives, you are never far from the family patterns that have become a part of each of you. What seems, for instance, to one of you the only way to celebrate Christmas may seem foreign to the other. The "child of the past" who lives within each of us longs for the familiar and, as noted earlier, may feel at home with some things the "adult of the present" professes to dislike. An awareness of this can make it easier for you to talk about your differences and adjust to them as you develop your own patterns of living.

Into the Wider Family

Whether we realize it or not, each of our small family units is part of a much wider extended family to which we belong, and for which we have some personal responsibility. This family consists not only of blood relatives and in-laws, but also fellow citizens in our local community and wider world. It is possible that we can become so involved with the political and social concerns of the community and nation that we neglect our specific responsibilities to spouse and children. But the opposite is also true; we can be so preoccupied with the inside business of the little family circle that we neglect our wider responsibilities to the community at large. When this happens it too may be detrimental to our personal relationships with husband, wife, parents, and children.

Here again it is true that we find our lives by losing them. If our total concern is to save the marriage and create a happy family, we may be so self-preoccupied and self-centered that we become increasingly difficult persons with whom to live. We all need to get out of ourselves and to find reasons for living beyond our personal or family self-preservation. A wise counselor once suggested to a troubled person, "Find someone who needs you and then give yourself to help that person," and when we are excessively wrapped up in ourselves, we do well to follow that advice. In one sense, the most important people in the world for each of us are not just those whom we need, but those who need us. Some of these are within the intimate circle of the little family, but others are served through agencies of church and community. As we give ourselves to this service, we not only help others but also discover new meaning for ourselves.

We especially urge you to seek friendships with persons in the older generation. There is sometimes less of a gap between grandparents and grandchildren than between parents and children. The idealism of youth and the wisdom of age can enable a meeting of hearts and minds which surprises everyone involved. Old age gives no guarantee of either insight or maturity, but we think that you will be enriched by exploring the possibilities of cross-generational giving and receiving. If there is some kind of Friendly Visitor program in your church or community which could bring you into specific relationship with a senior citizen or two, we invite you to check it out.

Faithfulness in Open Marriage

It must be obvious by now that we affirm the basic tenets of open marriage which seek to ensure personal fulfillment within the context of married love. In a healthy marriage, individuality and mutuality go together. We saw a beautiful symbol of this fact at a recent wedding. At the beginning of the ceremony, there were two candles burning at the front of the church with an unlit candle standing between them. After speaking their vows, the couple lit the center candle from each of the ones already burning but did not, as we have sometimes seen, blow out the individual candles. Had they done so, it would have seemed to us a sign of individuality going up in smoke. As the three candles continued to burn, it was a symbol of both the mutuality and the individuality, the unity and the diversity that characterize mature marriages.

While endorsing the basic principles of open marriage, we do not believe it is possible to have stability without a solid foundation of trust and faithfulness. It is one thing to say, "I'll attend the Bach recital while you are at the rock concert," but quite another to say, "You can go to bed with anyone you desire and I'll feel free to do the same." As we need room to grow in our personal interests, we also need limits to maintain the relationship.

In marriage we make a basic commitment of faithfulness to each other. We give ourselves to be special to each other. We declare each other to be first in our love and trust. As it is logically impossible to have two best friends, or two highest loyalties, we can't have a primary love commitment to two people at the same time. There are some who believe it is possible to maintain a basic love commitment while allowing all manner of extra-marital relationships, but we are either too old-fashioned or too wise to believe that. We cannot be special to each other while sharing everything with someone else.

Reading this, some might reply, "I agree, we are special to each other but why not be special in other ways? We will vow to always attend Bach recitals together but we may occasionally decide to go to bed with someone else or even to find our primary sexual fulfillment outside of marriage while finding our more basic personal fulfillment within it."

Sacramental Sex

Life is an exceedingly complex business and we do not wish personally to condemn others whose views or styles of living are different from our own, but we believe that sex is something special and that this is a fact not just of our culture but of our creation. Music is for public consumption; sex is for private communion. We believe that sexual relations are meant to be the personal sacrament of each marriage, and to share this gift with others is to undercut the foundations of the relationship and to cheapen the gift itself.

Sexual promiscuity either before or during marriage seems to us as unwise as it is immoral. Some say that a couple should test their sexual compatibility before marriage, but this kind of evaluation may be similar to testing a parachute by jumping from a fifth-story window. The conditions need to be right and in terms of sexual fulfillment that, for us, means the existence of a secure relationship of love and commitment. The fact that compatibility is being tested introduces elements of insecurity and fear of failure which undermine the test itself. Similarly in marriage, if promiscuity is sinful, it is also unwise and hurtful. One of us once talked with a person whose personal evaluation of an extra-marital affair was not, "How could I have been so wicked?" but rather, "How could I have been so stupid?" There are others who obviously regard their affairs differently. Some view them with gratitude and genuinely thank God for them, but we continue to believe that, in the vast majority of cases, they are destructive of the marriage relationship and in the long run filled with much more potential for misery than for joy.

To Be Trusted

While putting stress on sexual fidelity, we realize that there are hundreds of other ways to break faith with each other. We can fall so in love with our work, our money, our golf game or bridge club, even our children, that we have little time to care for each other. Some who develop an unhealthy dependence on alcohol or drugs are actually involved in a chemical love affair in which preoccupation with the chemical overshadows and threatens all other relationships. We can lie, deceive, and mislead in ways that make it next to impossible for us to trust each other. Trust is created by the persons in whom we have it, and while it takes much time to build, it can be quickly destroyed. As you wish to be trusted, seek to do everything you can to enable your partner, and everyone else for that matter, to trust you.

There may be some rare circumstances in life when it's necessary to lie to preserve a life (as when a World War II family told the Gestapo they had not seen the American paratrooper hidden in their home), or to keep a confidence (as when quizzed about information you have pledged to keep secret), but we should avoid deception, including all the white lies and half truths that undermine our ability to trust each other. Open sharing of the essential truth is a vital component of healthy open marriage.

A Faith to Share

Along with everything else, we are grateful to have been able to share a common faith and united experience of worship. We believe that God loves us even more than we love ourselves or could ever love each other and that he has promised to love us forever. We have done and will do many hurtful things, but in Jesus Christ we still dare to trust that nothing we have done or can do will ever stop God from loving us. As it is not possible for us to stop the sun from shining, so also we believe that it is impossible for us to stop God from loving us. This shared faith continues to give strength and meaning to our lives. Beyond this message of God's gracious love and power that is so basic to our central trust and hope, we are also continually refreshed by the human relationships within the wider family of our community of faith.

Both of us have come from homes in which Christian faith seemed a natural part of the fabric of life, but in neither of these families was there an abundance of religious ritual or a legalistic rigidity concerning either belief or behavior. The prevailing atmosphere was one in which we were encouraged to live with trust in a gracious God who was Christlike in love and mercy and to live with love toward people who, however much we might dislike or differ from them, were as loved and valued by God as we were ourselves.

We do not know how our children will someday look back on the spiritual dimension of our family life together, but our hope for you, as for them, is that you will be enabled to live your lives in trust of God and love of people and that you will be able to share this dimension of depth and height with one another.

Reverence the Mystery

As you live in trust of God you will be constantly called away from the kind of idolatrous dependence upon and worship of each other about which we warned you earlier. But at the same time you will experience an increased reverence for the mystery of life which you encounter in yourselves and in each other. After years of marriage, which will tempt you to believe you can read each other like a book, you will often be surprised by mystery that will make you say, "I couldn't understand you fully if we lived together for a hundred years"—and it will be true. Each of us human beings is a miniature world of mystery, perhaps more complex than all the physical universe.

Being unable fully to comprehend our wives or husbands should not really surprise us, for in fact we do not very well understand ourselves. We often wonder, "Why did I do that?" or "How could I have forgotten?" or "What makes me feel this way?" We are a mystery to ourselves as well as to one another.

A sense of mystery and bit of awe in each other's presence makes life a more exciting adventure. In our marriages such reverence for the mystery of life keeps us from settling down in the dull satisfaction of having arrived. In marriage, as in all of life, we never arrive; we are always on the way. We are on the move, hopefully, toward total marriage and total joy, but we are always far short of it. As the beauty of the swift, sparkling stream far excels the sight of a stagnant pond, so the gladness of life venturing, risking, stumbling, and rising to move on again by far exceeds the joy of life at rest. Thus may each day for you be an adventure of new beginning—a day full of danger and full of hope—a day full of grace and by that grace a day of life abounding.

The Best Year of Your Lives

Some time ago we received a letter from E. Stanley Jones which concluded with the words, "May you have the best year of your lives." This is our final wish for you as you begin your married life together, and on every wedding anniversary we want that wish to be automatically renewed for each new year ahead.

Having begun early in this letter by warning you to prepare for the worst, we end by urging you to be open to the best. Each of us needs some place to be at our worst, and home is probably the safest place for that—but home is also a good place for us to be at our best. Within the safety of marriage, you are free to give yourselves to each other in the abandonment of love.

Look for the best in each other, share your best with each other, give your best selves a chance to flower and to grow. You have potential for pain; we have said enough about that, but you also have great potential for pleasure and joy.

God in love wills to bless you and to give you life in all its fullness. May you so live in that love that your lives together may be to his glory and to your great joy.

With love,

Aunt Carol
and Uncle Lowell

Appendix: Questions for Reflection and Discussion

These questions are especially intended to encourage communication between men and women planning or experiencing marriage and for use in marriage enrichment groups. To stimulate focused discussion between engaged couples and spouses, and to facilitate concrete as well as comprehensive discussion in groups, they are presented under eight themes expressive of some of the most important concerns of persons married or soon to be. Page references to relevant sections of *Be Good to Each Other* are also included.

A. On Expectations (pp. 3–8):

1. What are the most significant characteristics of good and bad marriages?
2. What do a couple have a right to expect of each other? What have they no right to expect?
3. What do a couple have a right to expect of marriage? What have they no right to expect?

4. What portion of life's troubles and joys do you think come from being married? From factors unrelated to the marital state?

5. What do you consider the most significant factors contributing to fulfillment or lack of fulfillment in marriage? Why are these so important?

6. In what specific ways can realistic expectations help us avoid unnecessary frustration and disappointment?

7. How can we help each other to have more realistic expectations of marriage? Of ourselves? Of each other?

8. What can we do to help make our most positive expectations come true?

B. On Communication (pp. 9–19):

1. If it is true that to love is to share what is in your deepest heart, what do we have to share? Is it all good and beautiful?

2. Why do you think that it is so difficult for us to share the best and the worst of what is in us?

3. Do you agree that each of us yearns for a relationship in which we can be open and honest with each other? What can be done if one hungers for such sharing, but the other fears or feels little need of it?

4. Do you think that the mental and emotional intimacy of sharing mind and heart brings us even closer together than the physical intimacy of sexual relations? Why?

5. Some who claim to love truly find it difficult to say, "I love you." What do you think accounts for this? What can be done about it?

6. Can you give specific examples of ways by which we silence each other and cut off communication?

Specific examples of ways we help each other to be more expressive?

7. What are the dangers of relying on reading each other's mind? To what extent is verbal communication necessary? When is it enough to let our attitudes and actions speak for themselves?

8. How important are questions such as, "What do you mean?" and "What are you trying to tell me?"

9. Try using some of the communication starters such as "Honey, I . . ." games (p. 13). Can you suggest other specific means of increasing concrete communication?

10. Should a couple tell each other everything? Why? When?

11. Do you agree that is is best to "accentuate the positive"? Can we do so and yet be honest? How?

C. On Being Good Friends (pp. 21-30):

1. How important is it to "marry a good friend"? What are the signs and characteristics of such friendship?

2. What is the significance of mutual respect? To what extent is it important that marriage be a partnership of equals?

3. Why is pity a very poor basis for marriage?

4. In what ways is it possible to treat one's spouse as a kind of "god"? Why do you think this happens? In what ways is it dangerous? How can we correct such attitudes? 180975

5. What is your opinion of marriages in which one or both are committed to changing the other? Does acceptance or coercion make constructive change more likely? When is coercion necessary?

6. To what extent are "the pains of intimacy" a part of every relationship in depth? How can we help our-

selves and each other endure these pains constructively?

7. Could you be content with a good business-partner-
type marriage without the intimacy of close friendship? Explain.

8. What will result if both husband and wife think most
about what they can get from, rather than give to,
each other?

9. To what extent should "I'm sorry, Honey" be part of
the language of marriage? What effects does such
confession have? Can it be overdone?

10. How can vicious circles of meanness be broken and
new cycles of kindness be started? Can you give
examples?

11. Is it possible to live without angry and hostile feelings
toward each other? What happens when we try to do
so?

12. What is the difference between saying, "You make me
angry!" and "I am angry because the apartment is a
mess"? How can we do more confessing of our own
feelings and less accusing and attacking of each other?

13. What are the most constructive ways of handling
hostile feelings? What are the most destructive? How
can we express our anger more constructively?

D. On Decision-making (pp. 31–42):

1. Does the husband as "head of the house" have the
right to make all major decisions?

2. Does a wife who lets her husband make all major
decisions give up something essential to her whole
personhood?

3. Should husbands and wives give each other the right to make decisions in certain areas? Is such an arrangement the complete solution to problems of decision-making?

4. Do you agree that it is better for husbands and wives to think in terms of "What's right?" than "Who's right?" What are the advantages and disadvantages of this procedure?

5. Which of the tests of right and wrong on pp. 34–35 seem most important to you? Can you give examples of their use? Can you suggest other tests?

6. In what circumstances is it wise for a husband or wife to "give in" to the other? When is it unwise? What are the possible consequences of either action?

7. Why is it more helpful to concentrate on specific problems and possible solutions than to complain about each other's faults?

8. When is it wise to postpone making a decision? When is it unwise? What can a couple do when one or both can't make decisions?

9. What place do "I'll do something for you if you will do something for me" contracts have in marriage?

10. Is the "What's right?" rather than "Who's right?" approach in harmony with biblical passages such as Genesis 1:26-31; 2:18-25; I Corinthians 14:34-36; Galatians 3:27-28; Ephesians 5:21-33; I Timothy 2:8-15; and I Peter 3:1-7? Which of these most clearly express the gospel of Christ and which are more expressive of the culture and custom of that time?

11. Compare Ephesians 5:21-33 with Ephesians 6:5-9. If we do not understand 6:5-9 as an endorsement of slavery for all time, is it also possible that we need not understand 5:21-33 as an endorsement of male-dominated marriage for all time? Why?

E. On Sexual Fulfillment (pp. 43-51):

Discuss the truth or falsity of the following statements:
1. The most important purpose of sexual relations is to have children, the next is to express love, and the third is for personal pleasure. T____F____
2. I Corinthians 7:5 teaches us that sexual relations are not just for the purpose of having children. T____F____
3. Desire for sexual fulfillment is the number one reason for getting married. T____F____
4. Persons having strong sexual attraction for each other are most likely to have a successful marriage. T____F____
5. Persons with little sexual interest in each other should not get married. T____F____
6. Men are much more interested in sex than women. T____F____
7. Women are capable of greater sexual satisfaction than men. T____F____
8. The test of a sexual relationship is in its effect upon the total person. T____F____
9. Couples should not have sexual relations unless both are equally interested. T____F____
10. It is the husband's responsibility to initiate sexual overtures and the wife's to say Yes or No. T____F____
11. During sexual relations the husband should be active and the wife passive. T____F____
12. Christians are forbidden from engaging in other than "standard" sexual activity. T____F____
13. It's perfectly all right for Christian couples to do anything sexually which they both desire and enjoy. T____F____
14. It's sinful for a Christian couple to enjoy seeing an X-rated movie together. T____F____

15. The frequency of sexual relations decreases dramatically after the first year of marriage. T____F____
16. Many healthy couples continue an active sex life into their sixties, seventies, and eighties. T____F____
17. Genesis 1:27, 31 and 2:24-25 teach us that sex is good. T____F____
18. Since sexual relations are a sacramental gift from God, Christian couples should enjoy them often. T____F____
19. The Christian doctrine of grace speaks directly against attitudes that regard sexual relations as work or which demand performance of oneself or each other. T____F____
20. The message of grace invites us to approach each other in love without demanding anything of ourselves or each other. T____F____
21. Since most sexual problems can't be solved anyway, there is no use to talk with anyone about them. T____F____
22. In a fully open marriage, couples who love each other will give each other freedom to have sexual relations with whomever they wish. T____F____
23. Extra-marital affairs are not just against the Bible, but are against marriage and against each other. T____F____
24. Premarital sexual relations are okay between persons who really love each other. T____F____
25. One of the problems with premarital sexual relations is that they tend to short-circuit the relationship and hinder the development of friendship. T____F____
26. Couples who really love each other will usually refrain from sexual relations before marriage. T____F____
27. God did not give us the commandment forbidding

adultery because sex is evil, but because it is good. T____F____

28. The purpose of the commandment forbidding adultery is to help ensure sexual fulfillment and to preserve the family. T____F____
29. Jesus' statement that "everyone who looks at a woman lustfully has already committed adultery with her in his heart" (Matthew 5:28) condemns all sexual desire as evil. T____F____
30. Sexual desire is a gift of God and is as normal and good as blood pressure or hunger for food. T____F____
31. Lust is not the same as sexual attraction. T____F____
32. Words as well as actions are a very important part of a sexual experience. T____F____
33. All experiences of sexual relations are about the same. T____F____
34. Since sex is serious business, there is no place for humor in sexual relationships. T____F____
35. Some kinds of humor are destructive of a sexual relationship. T____F____

F. On Getting Out of Old Ruts (pp. 53–56):

1. Can you give examples to illustrate boredom and its effects in marriage?
2. What do you consider the most significant factors contributing to boredom in marriage? The factors preventing boredom?
3. How important is it for both husband and wife to plan activities together or to take turns in planning them? In what ways can contracting to do so be helpful?

4. Is it better to confess feelings of boredom to each other or to seek excitement elsewhere?

5. To what extent should we do things which are enjoyable and exciting to our partners, but which seem unnecessary or silly to us?

6. If honest self-examination reveals that we are bored with ourselves and life in general and not just with each other, what can we do to discover new meaning and joy in living?

7. In what circumstances should a couple seek outside counsel to improve their marriage? Should every couple promise each other, when first married, to seek outside counsel before filing for separation or divorce?

8. When is a husband or wife justified in seeking separation or divorce?

9. When contemplating separation or divorce of what significance are such questions as "Will this really solve my problems?" "Is this what I really want?" "Is there nothing further we can do to renew the relationship?"

10. What more might church, school, and state do to help make divorce less necessary?

11. Are divorce and remarriage of divorced persons in accord with biblical passages such as Matthew 5:31-32; Matthew 19:3-12; Mark 10:2-12; Luke 16:18; and 1 Corinthians 7:10-11?

12. Do Jesus' words "Not all men can receive this saying but only those to whom it is given . . . . He who is able to receive this, let him receive it" (Matthew 19:11-12) mean that Jesus' prohibitions of divorce and remarriage of divorced persons are not universal laws for all people for all time?

13. What are the implications of the Christian gospel of grace for specific decisions concerning divorce and remarriage of divorced persons?

G. On Relationships beyond Each Other (pp. 57–67):

1. Is it wrong for a couple to decide never to have any children? To have more than two or three children?
2. Are physically safe means of birth control a gift from God for which we give him thanks and praise?
3. When and why is abortion justified? When and why is it not justified?
4. Are children always a blessing to marriage?
5. How important is money in a marital relationship?
6. Should every couple have a specific budget, or is it enough that expenditures don't exceed income?
7. When both husband and wife work, is it better to keep separate accounts or to put the money together and have joint checking and savings accounts?
8. When both work, to what extent should they share household responsibilities? How are these best arranged?
9. What is the importance of play in our personal and married life? What can we do to enable and increase playfulness?
10. What is the significance of periodic weekends away together? How can these be economically arranged?
11. Of what importance is it to have outside friendships with individuals? With other couples? Are there dangers?
12. What are the most difficult problems in getting along with in-laws? What are the best ways of handling these problems?
13. Do you agree that if serious conflicts arise with in-laws each of you should take the central role in dealing with your own parents?
14. Are your in-law problems caused by overprotective, domineering parents, or by defensive, insecure

children? What can be done to establish a more adult-adult relationship?

15. If suggestions often imply criticism, can you illustrate some of the best and worst ways of giving advice?
16. Of what significance to marriage are relationships beyond the family circle?

H. On Faithfulness and Faith (pp. 69–75):

1. To what extent do you agree with the principles of "open marriage"? Give examples to illustrate your views.
2. In what ways is it sometimes necessary to sacrifice personal fulfillment for marital fulfillment? Marital fulfillment for personal fulfillment?
3. What is special about sexual relations? Can they be shared with others without damaging the marital relationship?
4. In what ways other than sexual infidelity can a husband and wife be unfaithful to each other?
5. What is necessary in marriage to enable a couple to trust each other? Do you agree that trust is created by the persons in whom we have it?
6. Are there times when it is best for couples to withhold the truth or to lie to each other?
7. In what ways does the mystery of each other's presence add frustration or fascination to marriage?
8. How important is it for a couple to share the spiritual dimensions of life? What are some of the better ways of handling the adjustments of a religiously mixed marriage?
9. Is it possible to share a common faith while belonging to different churches? What attitudes are essential to such a situation?

10. Is retreating into religious indifference a realistic solution to problems of religious differences?
11. Can you suggest specific means by which a couple can more fully share the spiritual dimensions of life?
12. What can a couple do to enable each other to look forward to sharing the coming years together?